For **Christian**. Embrace change. Be the change.
I love you, my best buddy!

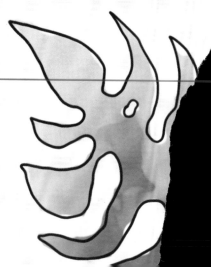

THE SiHEK

and the THING that was different

Written and Illustrated by **Frank U. Candaso, Jr.**

Edited by **Becky T. Toves**

On a warm and breezy Sunday on the island of Guam, a sihek was flying through the skies. He fluttered around, enjoying the wind rustling between his feathers as he soared along the horizon.

The sihek was young. He had just learned to fly and never flew beyond his home. But today, he wanted to explore.

As he flapped his wings faster and faster and flew higher and higher, from a distance the sihek noticed another being that was not like him scurrying across the land.

It was different. It wasn't orange or blue like him. It didn't have tints of red or cerulean. In fact, it looked a little bit dull with a dark shade of brown with black and white stripes that seemed to clash with the rest of its body. It wasn't flying. It had long legs. And it had a beak that was much longer than that of a sihek.

"What are you?" the sihek asked himself.
"You are definitely different from me."

Curious, he flew down toward the extraterrestrial to get a closer look and to determine what exactly this *thing* was.

The sihek perched on a tree branch and peered through the leaves just close enough to see the unfamiliar subject, but far away enough not to be seen.

He investigated. He observed this newfound creature, and he tried to make sense of what he was seeing.

Unable to identify this *thing*, the sihek decided to be kind and exclaimed, *"Håfa adai!"* to the animal.
In which it replied, *"Håfa adai!"*

Shocked, the sihek was flustered that this *thing* knew his language. *"How?"* he asked himself.

He wanted an even closer look and built up enough courage to move in and face this *thing*. He cautiously approached the foreigner, flew to the ground, and motioned his head downward to demonstrate that he meant no harm.

In return, the dark-brown-black-and-white-striped animal stood still and allowed the sihek to conduct his investigation.

"You have wings like me," the sihek proclaimed. "You're definitely a bird," he concluded as he determined what the *thing* was.

"That's right!" said the unknown bird. "I'm just like you, but I don't really fly. I'm afraid of heights to be honest."

"Afraid of heights?" the sihek asked confusedly,
"What bird is afraid of heights?"

As he flapped his wings faster and [...] flew higher and higher, from [...] another being that was [...] and [...] turned [...] across the [...]

"ME!" the bird exclaimed as it chuckled. "I am a ko'ko' bird and my family and I, we are flightless birds. That means we can't fly long distances like you."

"Iiiiiinteresting," the sihek thought. "How do you know my language then?"

"It's my language, too. It is possible to have the same language as you and still look different," the ko'ko' explained.

"I guess that is possible," the sihek said. "Then why are you different?"

The ko'ko' laughed. "It's okay to be different," it said. "Isn't the island more beautiful and interesting because of these differences? I saw you flying in the sky, but I did not think you were weird for not being like me."

"Come to think of it, I never thought of it that way," the sihek accepted. "You're right! It *is* an amazing thing to be different. It makes the *world* more interesting. It makes it colorful, just like me!"

"YES!" the ko'ko' said encouragingly. "There are many ways we are different, and many ways we can use our differences to *make* a difference in the world."

"I have an idea," the ko'ko' said.
"Follow me!"

15

The sihek followed the ko'ko' into a nearby jungle.
He didn't feel scared. He felt curious. He felt uncertain.
He felt unaware. He felt... excited. He wondered what
other *things* were out there and just how different they
could be.

As they approached the end of the trail, the sihek could
hear water gushing down a cliff and became
overwhelmed with as much emotion as the roaring of
the water falling.

The ko'ko' guided the sihek and separated a patch of
sword grass to reveal a whole new environment to the
sihek.

Flabbergasted, the sihek's eyes grew wide as he became elated with emotion and filled with curiosity. He saw other *things*. Other different, unique, and amazing *things*!

He saw a *hilitai.*

He saw a *haggan tåsi.*

He saw a *karabao.*

He saw an *ababang*.

The sihek realized they weren't just *things*—they were creatures just like him!
All with different features. All different types.
All different heights, and widths, and textures, and colors. From the land, to the sea, to the air. All... different. With each animal, or fish, or insect having qualities and *things* that made the jungle a wonderful place to live.

Even with their differences, all the animals were welcoming of the sihek. It didn't matter how he looked. They just naturally made him feel like he belonged, even if he didn't *look* like he belonged.

This made the sihek happy. And in that moment, he told himself he wouldn't be fearful of others based on their appearance, but that he would try to make them feel welcomed and loved no matter how they looked.

It was this message of kindness that the sihek would work to spread in his community; to embrace differences in others in order to make the island, and even the world, a special and extraordinary place to live.

CHamoru name: Sihek
Scientific name:
Todiramphus cinnamominus
English name:
Guam Kingfisher

The sihek is an endemic species. This means that this specific species of sihek is only found on Guam.

The Guam sihek male and female birds have different physical appearances. The male has a full cinnamon-colored body plumage, cerulean stripe near the eye, and cerulean wings. The female sihek is identified by its white body plumage.

The last wild Guam sihek was seen in 1988 and has since been declared extinct mainly due to the arrival of foreign and invasive species like the brown tree snake.

The sihek have been in captivity since 1984 with a population of only 140 that remain today.

Source:
Guam Department of Agriculture,
Division of Aquatic and Wildlife Resources
163 Dairy Road Mangilao, Guam 96913

Photo by Anthony J. Tornito

Hilitai
Monitor Lizard

Haggan tåsi
Sea Turtle

Ababang
Butterfly

Karabao
Water Buffalo

Sihek
Guam Kingfisher

Ko'ko'
Guam Rail

Håfa adai
Hello

Special thanks to:

Anthony J. Tornito and Laura Dueñas, Biologists, *DAWR*

Siñora Rufina Mendiola, Gisela Guile, Divina Leones-Tumanda, and Mr. Joseph Sanchez.

Darwin Vicente, Ron Ravela and Mawee Aguon
"The Publishing Team"